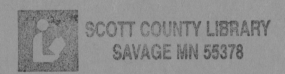

BIG BROTHER
HAS WHEELS

Written by Patrick "Packy" Mader
Illustrations by Andrew Holmquist

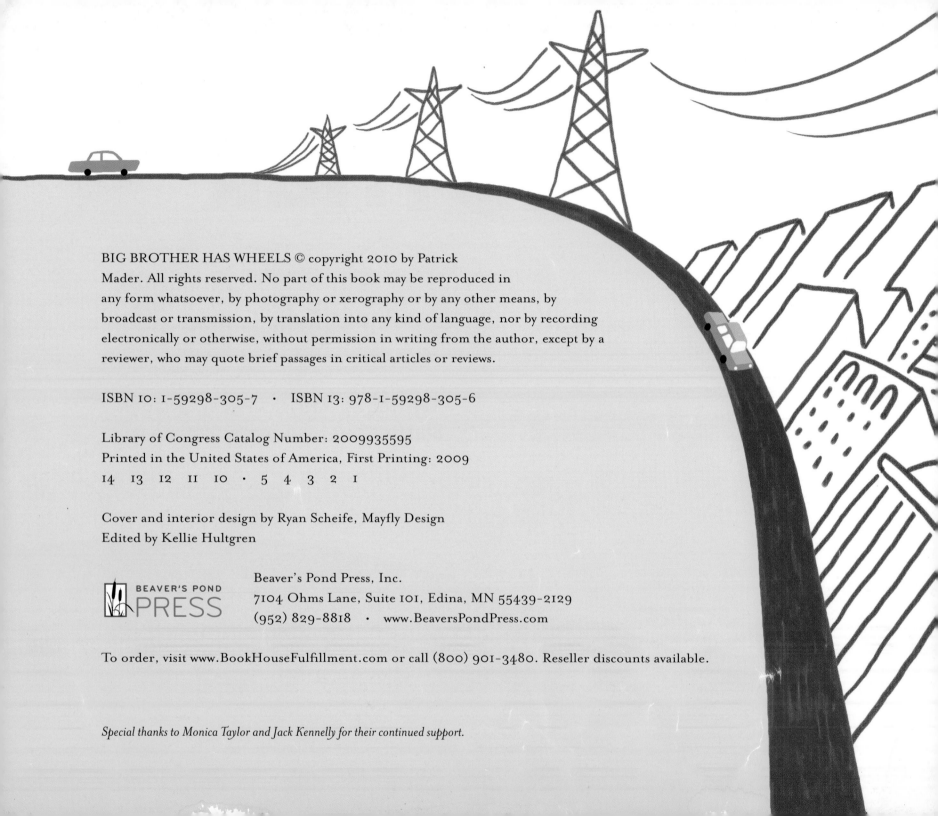

ISBN 10: 1-59298-305-7 · ISBN 13: 978-1-59298-305-6

Library of Congress Catalog Number: 2009935595
Printed in the United States of America, First Printing: 2009
14 13 12 11 10 · 5 4 3 2 1

Cover and interior design by Ryan Scheife, Mayfly Design
Edited by Kellie Hultgren

BEAVER'S POND PRESS

Beaver's Pond Press, Inc.
7104 Ohms Lane, Suite 101, Edina, MN 55439-2129
(952) 829-8818 · www.BeaversPondPress.com

To order, visit www.BookHouseFulfillment.com or call (800) 901-3480. Reseller discounts available.

Special thanks to Monica Taylor and Jack Kennelly for their continued support.

P.M.

To Jim and Jay
Beloved Big Brothers

Karen, Karl, and Ellen
Beloved wife, son, and daughter

A.H.

To my big brother Matt
and my parents Chris and Sue.

Thanks for teaching me
how to drive.

Big Brother liked wheels. He TURNED and SPUN the wheels on his toy trucks and tractors. He made tracks in the mud and snow.

Big Brother lived on a farm in Minnesota.
He EXPLORED the farm on his trike.
Sometimes he tied a wagon to his trike and pulled
loads of vegetables from the garden to the house.

His parents smiled and asked,
"What will Big Brother drive next?"

Big Brother grew and needed bigger wheels.
He rode his new bike beyond the farm.
He surprised his brothers and sisters when he showed them
hidden paths and ponds he had discovered on his adventures.

His brothers and sisters asked,
"What will Big Brother drive next?"

Soon, Big Brother learned to drive a tractor. He HAULED hay bales.
He gave his brothers and sisters rides on the hay wagon.
They BUMPED across the fields, past cows and tall corn plants.

"What will Big Brother drive next?" they wondered.

One summer, Big Brother got a driver's license. He took his brothers and sisters to places far from the farm in an old, rusty car.

They cheered at baseball games and swung wildly on green golf courses. They ate at restaurants in big cities and tasted new flavors of ice cream. They visited libraries and read about faraway places.

And the brothers and sisters asked each other, "What will Big Brother drive next?"

Big Brother got a job driving a machine called a forklift
at a toy factory. He scooted around corners with boxes of
toy dump trucks, bulldozers, and cranes. He loaded the toys
onto big trucks. Then the trucks hauled the toys to distant stores.
Even the toys were seeing the country.

Other workers waved as Big Brother honked the forklift's horn.
"What will Big Brother drive next?" they asked each other.

Then Big Brother bought his own car.
He named the copper-colored car "Minnesota Mama."
He took trips to many states. His brothers and sisters were
proud that Big Brother had his own wheels.
And so were his parents.

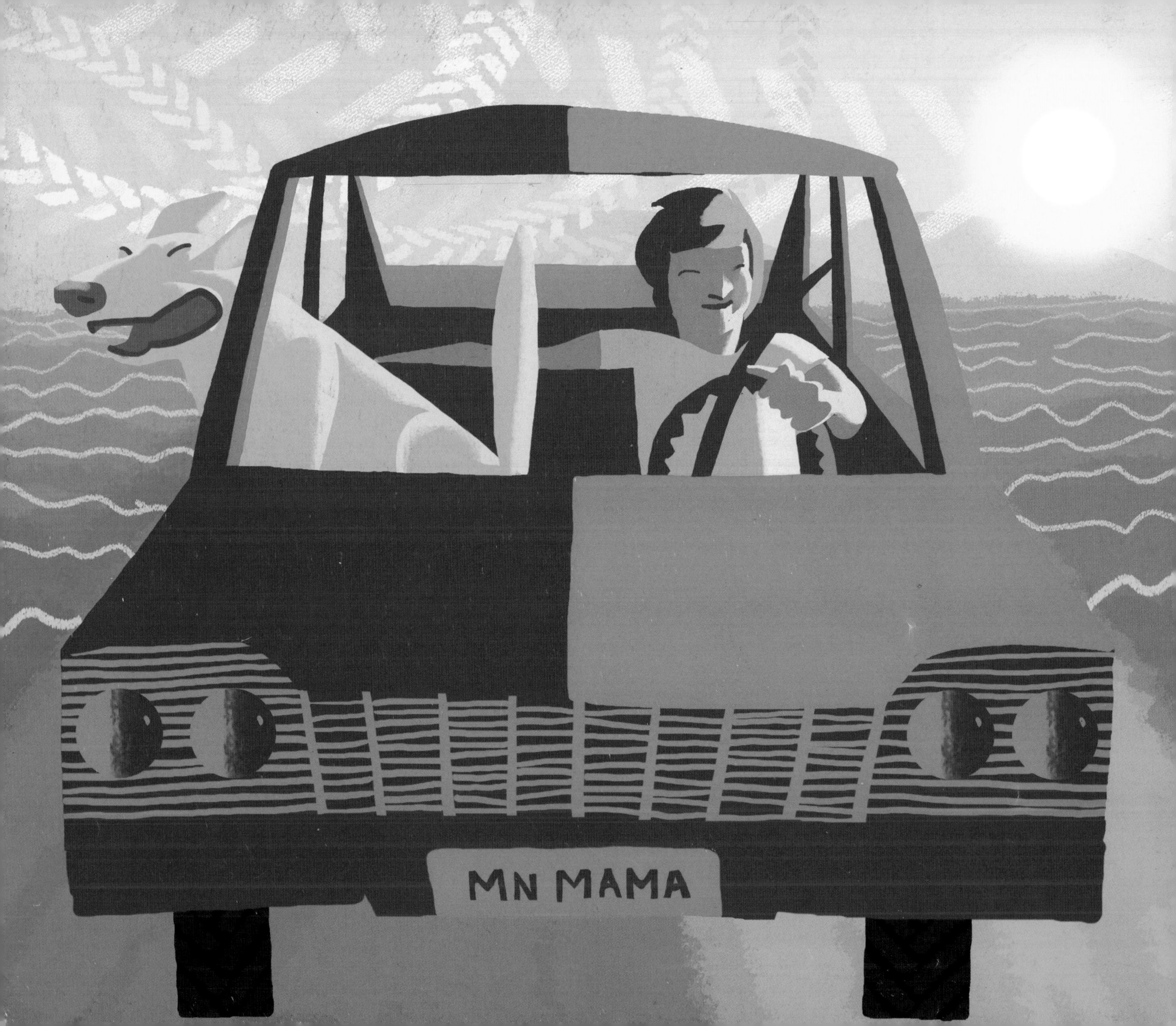
MN MAMA

The family liked riding in Minnesota Mama,
but the farm dog loved it! He hung his head out of the window
and let the wind flap his ears.

At night, the dog jumped onto the hood of Minnesota Mama,
walked up the windshield, and lay down on the roof.
And then he went to sleep.

In his dreams he wondered, "What will Big Brother drive next?"

Big Brother studied hard at college, but he also had fun driving new kinds of wheels. He **roared** around on a motorcycle. He *ZIPPED* by on a go-cart. In the winter, he swept across fields of snowdrifts on a snowmobile.

After college, Big Brother got a job in North Carolina, far away from the farm. He drove Minnesota Mama past cities with tall towers. The car went up and down curving mountain roads. Finally, he came to a stop at the shining ocean.

Then Big Brother took a long trip from North Carolina
to visit friends in the state of Washington.
He drove Minnesota Mama from coast to coast!

On the trip, he saw lots of wheels. He watched race cars *ZOOM*
around a track in Indiana. He saw parking lots full of motor homes
in South Dakota. He even saw a double-decker bus!

On the way, Big Brother stopped to visit his family at the farm.
His parents and brothers and sisters were very happy to see him.

And the dog was very happy to see Minnesota Mama.

"What will Big Brother drive next?" the family wondered
as they waved good-bye.

Later, Big Brother got married. He and his wife had five girls.
Now Big Brother drove a **NOISY** van. It was noisy because
the girls sang whenever Big Brother drove. And they sang loudly.

Sometimes the wheels would really ROCK and ROLL!

But the five girls grew and got their own wheels,
so Big Brother sold the **NOISY** van.

Everyone wondered, "What will Big Brother drive next?"

Soon Big Brother will be a grandpa. He hopes to share his love of wheels with his grandchildren. Wheels take him to places all over the country. They may take his grandchildren on adventures all over the world!

So everyone still wonders, "What will Big Brother drive next?"

Would you believe, a tiny convertible?

And...

a **PACKED** golf cart?

Patrick "Packy" Mader is an
elementary teacher who lives in
Northfield, Minnesota, with his
wife and two children. *Big Brother Has
Wheels* joins his other books, *Opa &
Oma Together* and *Oma Finds a Miracle*
as intergenerational stories that
celebrate rural lifestyles.

For more information about his
books and his background, please
visit **www.patrickmader.com.**

Andrew Holmquist received his
BFA from the School of the Art
Institute of Chicago. He grew up
in Minnesota and now lives in
Chicago where he draws and paints,
among other things. As often as he
can, Andrew uses wheels of all kind
to take him on adventures around
the world.